SU...
FUN-DAY!

Written by Judy Katschke
Illustrated by Artful Doodlers

SCHOLASTIC INC.

All rights reserved. Published by Scholastic Inc., *Publishers since 1920.*
SCHOLASTIC and associated logos are trademarks and/or registered trademarks of
Scholastic Inc.

ISBN 978-1-338-15899-1

10 9 8 7 6 5 4 3 2 1   17 18 19 20 21

Printed in the U.S.A.   40

First printing 2017

Book design by Erin McMahon

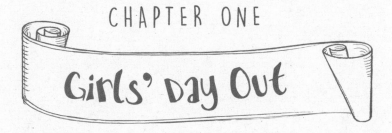

CHAPTER ONE

Girls' Day Out

"Check it out, girls," Jessicake said as she held out her tray proudly. "Four cupcakes with four kinds of frosting."

"Don't forget the hot cocoa, Jessicake," Donatina said, "with minidonuts on top!"

"Ooh! My cocoa has lots of minigumballs," Bubbleisha said, reaching for her cocoa cup. "Just the way I like it."

Jessicake tapped her chin thoughtfully. "There's just one thing missing," she said slowly.

"Missing?" Donatina repeated.

"What?" Bubbleisha asked.

"Not what . . . who," Jessicake replied.

"Peppa-Mint isn't here yet!"

Where was Peppa-Mint? Jessicake, Donatina, and Bubbleisha were too busy wondering to notice her standing a few feet away.

"Um . . . hello?" Peppa-Mint said quietly. "May I interrupt . . . please?"

"Where could she be?" Jessicake wondered.

"It was Peppa-Mint's idea to have a Girls' Day Out," Bubbleisha pointed out. "It's not like her to not show up."

"May I have your attention? Please?" Peppa-Mint called shyly. "Um . . . with sprinkles and cherries on top?"

"I'm the one who's usually late," Donatina said. Everyone's eyes were still on Peppa-Mint's empty chair.

"Everybody—freeze!" Peppa-Mint shouted.

Jessicake, Donatina, and Bubbleisha turned to see a blushing Peppa-Mint. It wasn't like their friend to shout—unless it was for ice cream!

"I didn't mean to yell," Peppa-Mint said softly, approaching the table with Carla Cone and Icy-Bowl. "But our Girls' Day Out . . . um . . . will now be held at the Cool Dream Ice Cream Parlor."

Jessicake, Donatina, and Bubbleisha stared at Peppa-Mint with surprise.

"The Cool Dream Ice Cream Parlor?" Jessicake asked. "But we all agreed on cupcakes today, Peppa-Mint."

"Why the switcheroo?" Bubbleisha asked.

"I just got a sad scoop," Peppa-Mint explained unhappily. "Because of all the yummy new snacks popping up all over Shopville, Cool Dream is losing customers!"

"You mean ice-cream sales are down?" Jessicake asked.

"You mean they may close the store?" Bubbleisha gasped.

"Forever and ever?" Donatina asked.

"Maybe." Peppa-Mint gulped. "No more Cool Dream would be my worst nightmare!"

Carla Cone and Icy-Bowl were especially worried.

"We think Peppa-Mint is on the verge of a meltdown," Carla Cone whispered to the Shoppies.

"And nobody likes a meltdown," Icy-Bowl whispered.

"Unless you're making s'mores," Donatina pointed out.

"I think we should help Peppa-Mint," said Bubbleisha. "But how?"

Jessicake thought for a moment, then smiled. "The way to help Peppa-Mint," she said, "is to help her cause!"

In a flash, the girls were by Peppa-Mint's side with words of encouragement.

"Maybe you need to do something big," Bubbleisha said, blowing a super-size bubble that burst with a *POP*. "Like that!"

"Maybe think out-side the box, Peppa-Mint," Jessicake sug-gested.

"Thanks, girls," said Peppa-Mint. "You're right. I have to come up with a way to bring business back to Cool Dream."

As she thought, Peppa-Mint gazed at the colorful cupcakes on the café table. An espe-cially sparkly one caught her eye.

"Um . . . excuse me?" Peppa-Mint asked, "but those sprinkles on that cupcake . . . are they . . . silver?"

"Not only are they silver," Coco Cupcake said, "Jessicake designed the toppings herself."

"It's what all well-dressed cupcakes will be wearing this year at the Cupcake Queen Café!" Cherry Cake declared.

Peppa-Mint's eyes lit up. "That's it!" she cried.

"What's it?" her friends asked together.

Peppa-Mint pumped an excited fist in the air and shouted, "Get ready, Shopville, for the first and best ice cream–inspired fashion show—"

Suddenly realizing how loud she was being, Peppa-Mint paused and continued softly, "ever."

CHAPTER TWO

Something Sketchy

"An ice-cream fashion show?" Bubbleisha asked.

"Awesome!" Donatina declared, then frowned in confusion. "What's an ice-cream fashion show?"

"I'll design outfits that look like ice-cream treats," Peppa-Mint explained. "And we can hold a fashion show at the Cool Dream Ice Cream Parlor! That should attract lots of new customers!"

"Sweet!" Jessicake exclaimed. "A fashion show is a definite must-have for Shopville."

"Tell us more, tell us more," Bubbleisha urged.

Peppa-Mint's minty-green eyes lit up as she said, "I'll call my line of clothes Float Couture . . .

after my favorite ice-cream soda!"

"Love!" Jessicake, Donatina, and Bubbleisha squealed.

"And I'd love for you to be my models!" Peppa-Mint added.

"Love more!" the girls exclaimed.

Peppa-Mint scooped up Icy and Carla, then turned and took off.

"Where are you going, Peppa-Mint?" Jessi-cake called.

"To brainstorm fashion ideas," Peppa-Mint

called back. "Meet me at the Small Mart tomorrow morning for the big reveal!"

Jessicake, Donatina, and Bubbleisha couldn't wait to see their friend's fashion ideas—and model in her fashion show.

"We're going to walk down the runway!" Bubbleisha cheered.

Donatina tilted her head. "If it's a runway . . . shouldn't we be running down it?" she asked.

"We'll figure it out, Donatina," Jessicake replied, patting her friend on the arm. "Until then—we'll figure out how to help Peppa-Mint

make this the best fashion show Shopville has ever seen!"

*   *   *   *   *

The next morning, Jessicake, Donatina, and Bubbleisha couldn't get to the Small Mart fast enough.

"I'm sure Peppa-Mint's sketches are awesome," Jessicake exclaimed.

But when the girls entered the store, something didn't seem right. The Shopkins looked

glad to see them, but they were not smiling.

"Thank goodness you're here!" said Apple Blossom.

"It's the pits, girls." Peachy groaned. "The absolute pits."

"What do you mean?" Bubbleisha asked.

"Is it Peppa-Mint?" Jessicake demanded.

"How did her fashion sketches come out?" Donatina asked.

"Let's just say she's got some work to do," Apple Blossom replied. "See for yourself."

The Shoppies turned to see where Apple Blossom was pointing. At the end of the aisle were three towering stacks of papers.

"Where is Peppa-Mint?" Bubbleisha asked.

Suddenly, out from behind the stacks peeked a bleary-eyed Peppa-Mint. Her hair was frazzled, and her mouth turned down in a frown.

"Um . . . hi," Peppa-Mint squeaked.

Jessicake, Donatina, and Bubbleisha raced toward their friend and the towering stacks.

"Look at all the sketches Peppa-Mint made!" Jessicake exclaimed. "I'm sure they're all—"

"Blank," Bubbleisha finished, staring at one of the papers. "This one is totally blank."

"So is mine," Donatina said, holding up a sheet.

"Oh, no!" Jessicake gasped as they flipped through piles of papers. "All of these papers are blank!"

"That's not all that's blank." Peppa-Mint said. "So is my mind!"

Jessicake, Donatina, and Bubbleisha watched as Peppa-Mint laid her head in her hands and groaned.

"Peppa-Mint, what happened?" Jessicake asked.

"Wasn't your brain supposed to storm?" Donatina asked.

"There's been a change in the forecast," Peppa-Mint wailed. "My brainstorm is now a brain freeze!"

Blank papers flew all about as Peppa-Mint jumped up. Without a word, she dashed away from the drawing board and out of the Small Mart.

"I've never seen Peppa-Mint so stressed," Icy admitted.

"Something tells me we have a long and rocky road ahead of us," Carla said with a sigh.

Refusing to be glum, the girls traded looks of determination.

"I like to see the chocolate-milk glass half full," Donatina declared, "not half empty!"

"When life throws you lemons, make chewy sour lemon drops!" Bubbleisha said with a smile.

"We all know that Peppa-Mint can design her Float Couture," Jessicake said. "She just has to snap out of her creative dry spell."

"And if anyone can help her do that," Bubbleisha piped in, "it's her friends!"

CHAPTER THREE

Shoppies Say Relax!

Jessicake, Donatina, and Bubbleisha headed to Donatina's Donut Delights to do some brain-storming of their own.

"Okay, girls," Jessicake said. "How can we help Peppa-Mint?"

Bubbleisha chewed on her gum while she racked her brain. She blew a big pink bubble that popped—and so did an idea!

"If we want to help Peppa-Mint," Bubbleisha said, "we have to think like Peppa-Mint."

"That means think ice cream-y," Donatina decided.

"In that case," Jessicake said slowly, "how

would we keep a scoop of ice cream from having a meltdown?"

"By chilling it," said Donatina.

"Which means," Bubbleisha said, "Peppa-Mint needs to chill! We have to help her relax!"

"Correct," Jessicake said with a smile. "And I think I know how!"

* * * * *

"Excuse me . . . but where are we going?" Peppa-Mint asked. "All I wanted to do was stay in bed . . . and eat bowls of mint-chocolate

chip . . . butter pecan . . . caramel crunch . . . banana fudge swirl . . ."

Icy-Bowl and Carla Cone both smiled as they led Peppa-Mint through Shopville. When they reached Donatina's Donut Delights, they came to a stop.

"We have reached our destination!" Carla said.

"Or should I say . . . *rest*ination?" Icy asked, chuckling at her own joke.

"Rest-ination?" Peppa-Mint repeated. She stared at the donut shop, wrinkling her nose in confusion. "Um . . . what happened to the sign for Donatina's Donut Delights?"

"We're not here for donuts," Icy said.

"Then why are we here?" Peppa-Mint asked.

"There's only one way to find out," Carla said cheerily. "Follow us!"

Upon entering the shop, Peppa-Mint did not smell the usual scent of donuts, powdered sugar, and jelly. Instead, the place smelled like—

"Lavender," Peppa-Mint said, taking a whiff. "Lemongrass . . . um . . . and excuse me, but is that patchouli?"

Peppa-Mint didn't see any donuts, either. Instead there were rows of flameless candles, sheer white curtains, and pillows on the floor. Perched on the pillows were Shopkins.

"Um . . . excuse me?" Peppa-Mint asked. "What's going on here?"

"It's yoga!" Fasta Pasta said with a smile.

"This pose is called the pretzel!" Pretz-elle said. "I'm a natural, don't you think?"

"Okay . . . I don't mean to be rude," Peppa-Mint said softly. "But where am I?"

Two curtains parted and out stepped Jessi-cake, Donatina, and Bubbleisha. Each girl wore a sherbet-colored smock and a smile. Stepping out after the girls were Lippy Lips, Polly Polish, Mindy Mirror, and Blushy Brush.

"Welcome, Peppa-Mint!" Donatina declared.

"Welcome where?" Peppa-Mint asked.

Jessicake raised a hand with a flourish. "Welcome to the Sweet Serenity Spa!"

CHAPTER FOUR

Bubble Trouble

"Spa?" Peppa-Mint exclaimed.

"The best way to bubble up those creative juices," Bubbleisha explained, "is to chillax!"

"And dollars to donuts, the best place to chillax is at a spa," Donatina said. "Right?"

More Shopkins stepped forward.

"May I suggest a rejuvenating peel?" asked Apple Blossom.

"An invigorating salt scrub?" Sally Shakes suggested.

"Aqua-therapy?" Wally Water asked.

Before Peppa-Mint could protest, she was wrapped mummy-style in white, fluffy towels from head to toe.

"That's a wrap!" Donatina said when they were done.

"Relaxed yet?" Bubbleisha asked Peppa-Mint.

"Sorry . . . but no," Peppa-Mint squeaked out beneath her towel cocoon. "I'm just not the spa type."

"This isn't just any spa," Jessicake said. "It's a candy, cookies, and cocoa spa."

"With *sweet*ments instead of treatments!" Donatina added.

"Sweetments?" Peppa-Mint asked. *Could ice cream be on the spa menu, too?* She wondered.

"Um . . . actually," Peppa-Mint said, "maybe I'm more the spa type than I thought."

Peppa-Mint agreed to a soothing and refreshing sugar cookie–scented bubble bath, courtesy of Bubbleisha.

Once in the tub, Peppa-Mint smiled and said, "Mmm . . . the water is nice and warm. But . . . I don't smell sugar cookies."

"You will soon," Bubbleisha said as she held up a rosy-colored bottle. "This sugar cookie bubble bath is my own supersecret formula."

"While Bubbleisha pours the bubbles, Polly will give you a complimentary pedicure," Jessi-cake said.

"Nice," Peppa-Mint said, leaning back in the tub. "I feel chilled already."

Slowly, Bubbleisha tipped the bottle over the tub. Peppa-Mint took a long, luxurious whiff of the sugar cookie–scented bubble bath as it rained gently into the warm water.

Polly began the pedicure, one toe at a time.

"This little piggy went to market," Polly said,

skillfully painting Peppa-Mint's littlest toe in mint green. "This little piggy stayed home . . ."

Peppa-Mint gasped as Polly worked on her next toe, then the next, then the next. Uh-oh! She had forgotten to tell everyone she was ticklish!

"Um, you guys . . ." Peppa-Mint chuckled. "That tickles . . . like . . . a lot!"

Polly was too busy polishing to hear. Peppa-Mint tried hard not to move, but when Polly got to the piggy who ate roast beef—

"Hahahahaha!" Peppa-Mint squealed.

Water and bubbles splashed everywhere as Peppa-Mint kicked her tickled feet up and down—until one kick sent the bubble bath bottle flying out of Bubbleisha's hand!

"Oh, nooooo!" Bubbleisha gasped.

The bottle dropped into the tub, emptying all of the bubble bath into the water. It wasn't long before Peppa-Mint was totally buried in bubbles!

"Um . . . this can't be good," Peppa-Mint called out from underneath. "Um . . . help?"

The Shopkins sprung into action. They had to get her out from under all those bubbles. Luckily, Polly Polish had an idea.

"Blow-Anne," Polly shouted. "You're on!"

Blow-Anne's blades spun and spun until— *SWOOSH*—the bubbles were blasted away from Peppa-Mint and all over Jessicake, Donatina, and Bubbleisha!

"Oops," Blow-Anne gulped. "I got a little carried away."

Underneath the bubbles, the girls agreed: The sugar cookie–bubble bath was an epic fail. But there were still plenty of other ways to help Peppa-Mint relax!

"Peppa-Mint," Jessicake's voice said calmly beneath the popping bubbles, "it is time to face your next sweetment."

CHAPTER FIVE

Face It!

Peppa-Mint gulped as her friends led her to the next curtain. "Um . . . I'm afraid to ask," she said. "But what's my next sweetment?"

"Nothing less than an awesomely refreshing face mask," Jessicake said excitedly.

"A mask?" Peppa-Mint asked. "But it's not Halloween . . . um . . . is it?"

"No." Bubbleisha chuckled. "And there'll be no tricks—just treats."

Bubbleisha flung open the curtain. Behind it was a cushy chair. Next to the chair was a small table holding a white ceramic jar.

Before Peppa-Mint could say "cherry-vanilla-chocolate-chip," Jessicake was gently pushing her back onto the chair so she was lying down.

While Jessicake mixed the concoction in the ceramic pot, Peppa-Mint took a deep breath and tried to clear her mind.

"Relax, Peppa-Mint," Jessicake said soothingly as she slathered thick cream all over her friend's forehead, cheeks, and chin. "This mask is sure to invigorate and inspire."

The mask felt creamy—what was that smell? Vanilla? Buttercream? Peppa-Mint flicked her

tongue, sneaking a lick. "Yum," she said. "Is this cupcake frosting?"

"C-c-c-cupcake?" Jessicake repeated.

Jessicake dropped the spoon with a *CLUNK*. Her eyes became distant as she stared at Peppa-Mint's frosty face.

"Is it . . . something I said?" Peppa-Mint cried.

Donatina shook her head and said, "When Jessicake thinks cupcake frosting—"

"She goes into decorate mode!" Bubbleisha finished.

Her eyes whirling with creative ideas, Jessicake whipped out more pots and jars. She fell into a topping frenzy, decorating Peppa-Mint's face as if it were a cupcake.

"Sprinkles! Candy-confetti! Coconut! Chocolate chips!" Jessicake cried as she added more

and more. It was as if she were back at the Cupcake Queen Café during the midafternoon sugar rush!

Donatina and Bubbleisha gently pulled Jessicake away from her candied creation.

"But I'm not finished," Jessicake protested. "It needs more toppings! It needs squiggly licorice gummy worms!"

"Worms?" Peppa-Mint cried, jumping out of the chair. She looked at Mindy Mirror and yelped even louder. "Ahhh! I've got cupcake face!"

"Okay, Jessicake," said Bubbleisha, grabbing a nearby glass, "snap out of it!" She splashed water on Jessicake's surprised face.

That seemed to do the trick. "I'm sorry, Peppa-Mint," Jessicake said as she dried her own drippy face with a towel. "But when I work with cupcake frosting, I go a little bananas . . ."

Jessicake's eyes began spinning again, "Bananas! That topping would go perfectly with—"

"Don't go there, Jessicake," Bubbleisha cut in.

"It's okay, Jessicake." Peppa-Mint sighed. "Um . . . I actually have a confession to make."

"You do?" Jessicake asked.

"What?" Bubbleisha wanted to know.

"It's just that . . . I don't think this is working. The last thing I want to do is work on my silly Float Couture!" Peppa-Mint wailed.

Jessicake, Donatina, and Bubbleisha traded frantic looks. Was Peppa-Mint on the verge of a meltdown? Luckily, the girls still had one more trick up their sleeves.

"Speaking of float," Donatina said with a smile, "wait till you see what's up next!"

CHAPTER SIX

No Tank-you

When Peppa-Mint saw what was behind the next curtain she was skeptical. "Is that . . . another tub?" she asked.

"It's a tank, actually," Donatina said excitedly. "My super-chillaxing Hole-istic Flotation Tank!"

Peppa-Mint stepped up to the tank and looked inside. "Is it filled with milk?" she asked.

"Yes, and Milk Bud helped!" Donatina said. She stuck two fingers in her mouth and gave a loud, shrill whistle.

"Woof!" Milk Bud barked, scurrying over.

"Fetch the donut, Milk Bud!" Jessicake said. "That's a good boy!"

"Donut?" Peppa-Mint repeated.

Milk Bud shot off. In the shake of a tail, the peppy pup was back bouncing an inflatable donut raft on his nose. With another bark, Milk Bud bounced the blow-up donut into the tank with a *SPLASH!*

"Well," Peppa-Mint said, gazing into the tank. "It does look relaxing, and I do like floating on rafts." She gave a nod and said, "Okay, I'm in!"

Jessicake, Donatina, and Bubbleisha cheered as Peppa-Mint climbed aboard the donut raft.

"Now, think happy thoughts," Donatina said in a singsong tone. "Drift away to your happiest place."

Closing her eyes, Peppa-Mint filled her mind with pistachio ice cream in waffle cones, butter-scotch sundaes with candied walnuts, and ice-cream sandwiches.

But her happy thoughts were interrupted when a voice shouted, "Is that milk?"

"A *hole* lot of milk!" another voice exclaimed.

Peppa-Mint's eyes popped open to see Daisy Donut and Rolly Donut perched on the rim of the tank.

"This must be our lucky day!" Rolly said.

"Hey, you guys," Daisy called. "Everybody in the pool!"

Peppa-Mint gasped as dozens more donuts appeared—taking running jumps to dive into the milk-tank!

"Nooooo!" Donatina cried as plain, frosted, and glazed donuts splashed around Peppa-Mint.

"Donatina!" Peppa-Mint shouted from the donut-filled tank. "Is this part of the sweet-ment?"

"Sorry, Peppa-Mint," Donatina wailed. "I forgot that when donuts see milk, they have to dunk."

"Plain old dunking is bor-ing!" Daisy Donut announced. "Synchronized swimming, anyone?"

"Oh, dear," Peppa-Mint said as her raft began to bob and tip from all the movement.

"Okay, I don't want to be a downer," Donatina whispered, "but something tells me this sweet-ment isn't working."

"For sure," Jessicake whispered. "And after putting Peppa-Mint through all this, we have to make it up to her."

"Good idea," Bubbleisha agreed. "But how?"

* * * * *

"Okay, Peppa-Mint," Jessicake said later, "we admit that things at the Sweet Serenity Spa were not exactly sweet."

Peppa-Mint nodded as she walked with her friends through Shopville. She had dried off and calmed down after her relaxing milk bath had gone sour. But where were Jessicake, Donatina,

and Bubbleisha taking her now?

"So what do you have in store for me next?" Peppa-Mint asked, trying to stay positive.

"What's in store—is a store!" Bubbleisha said. "The Fashion Spree!"

Peppa-Mint blinked her minty-green eyes. "You mean . . . you're taking me shopping?" she gasped.

A team of stylish Shopkins stood in front of The Fashion Spree ready to greet Peppa-Mint. She was happy for a little retail therapy. And the Shopkins were happy to help!

"How about some shiny new lip glosses, Peppa-Mint?" Lippy Lips asked, "They come in ten ice-cream flavors."

"Ooooh!" Peppa-Mint swooned happily.

"Or a new handbag?" Handbag Harriet asked. "Shady Diva says silver is the new black."

"I don't know where to start!" Peppa-Mint admitted excitedly as she looked around The Fashion Spree. "So I'll start at the top—with hats!"

Jessicake, Donatina, and Bubbleisha smiled as they watched Peppa-Mint race toward the hat section. Not only was their friend relaxed, but she also seemed to have forgotten all about her Float Couture!

"Look!" Peppa-Mint called as she happily pulled a super-fancy hat off the rack. "This hat reminds me of a cherry-vanilla hot-fudge sundae with nuts and whipped cream!"

Peppa-Mint smiled, placing the ice-cream

sundae–style hat on her head. She was about to look for a mirror when her eyes began to glow and grow!

"What's happening to Peppa-Mint?" Donatina whispered.

"Her eyes are as big as gumballs," Bubbleisha whispered. "The jumbo kind."

Jessicake smiled. She had seen that look on Peppa-Mint's face before.

"Girls," Jessicake whispered, "I think Peppa-Mint's brain freeze is about to melt!"

"That's it, that's it!" Peppa-Mint cheered, tossing the hat in the air.

"What's it?" Jessicake asked.

"I know how to make my ice cream–inspired fashions even better," Peppa-Mint explained. "I'll top off the outfit with super-stylish hats—made out of REAL ice cream!"

"Awesome!" the girls shouted.

Bubbleisha nudged Jessicake and whispered under her breath, "And what could possibly go wrong with that?"

CHAPTER SEVEN

Sundae Fun-Day

Lickety-split, the four friends were at the Cool Dream Ice Cream Parlor. But this time, they didn't go to eat ice cream—they went to work on Peppa-Mint's new line of real ice-cream fashions!

"Ooooh!" the Shopkins exclaimed with each outfit Peppa-Mint sketched. "Aaaaahhh!"

Jessicake, Donatina, and Bubbleisha happily helped, scooping ice cream to use for Peppa-Mint's hat designs. When the frozen fashions were done, the friends modeled them for Peppa-Mint: Banana Split Knit, Capes Suzette, and Frozen Dessert Maxiskirt, plus the matching

bowls of ice-cream sundaes as decorative hats.

Peppa-Mint stepped back to study her work.

"The cherry vanilla and strawberry," Peppa-Mint asked slowly. "Too matchy-matchy?"

"No way!" Jessicake, Donatina, and Bubble-isha said in unison.

"Okay, then!" Peppa-Mint cheered excitedly. "My line of Float Couture is ready to hit the run-way! And soon the Cool Dream Ice Cream Parlor will be a big hit!"

* * * * *

"Slow down, Peppa-Mint!" Bubbleisha called.

"It's crazy-hot today," Jessicake said.

"Donuts-fresh-out-of-the-oven hot!" Donatina declared.

Peppa-Mint couldn't slow down. She was too excited! It was the morning of her Float Couture fashion show at the Cool Dream Ice Cream Parlor, and she couldn't wait to get there.

"Hot is perfect for ice cream," Peppa-Mint called back excitedly. "And a real ice-cream fashion show!"

Peppa-Mint wasn't the only one in Shopville excited about the show. The girls were soon surrounded by the inquisitive Ice-Pop-arrazi.

"Give us the scoop, Peppa-Mint," Snow Crush shouted.

"Yes, Peppa-Mint," Popsi Cool said. "How would you describe your line of real ice-cream fashions?"

"Uh . . . tasteful?" Peppa-Mint suggested.

"Thanks, everyone," Jessicake told the reporters with a smile. "But Peppa-Mint can't wait to check out the runway."

"Um . . . yes," Peppa-Mint said. "Carla and Icy promised to set it up first thing this morning."

"You don't have to wait," Popsi Cool said, "because there it is!"

"Huh?" Peppa-Mint said, looking puzzled. She followed the reporters' gazes to the Cool Dream Ice Cream Parlor. Standing outside the shop was a red-carpeted fashion runway!

"Outside?" Donatina asked.

"Wasn't the runway supposed to be inside

the shop? It's much cooler in there," Jessicake pointed out.

"It's okay," Peppa-Mint said with a smile. "Outside means more room, and more room means more guests . . . right?"

As they approached the runway, it seemed Peppa-Mint was right. Seated on either side of the runway were Shopkins from every corner in Shopville!

The four friends hurried

backstage to get ready. Even Peppa-Mint would model her own Float Couture creations in the show.

"Let's go, girls!" Peppa-Mint squealed. She pointed to the freezer holding their Float Couture outfits, including the ice-cream-bowl hats. "And don't forget to accessorize."

Dressed to chill and holding their sundaes, Jessicake, Donatina, Bubbleisha, and Peppa-Mint peeked out from behind the curtain.

"Look!" Peppa-Mint whispered. "Shady Diva is stepping up to the podium!"

"*Bienvenue*, Shopville!" Shady said to thunderous applause. "And welcome to Mademoiselle Peppa-Mint's Float Couture fashion show where la mode . . . eez à la mode!"

Runway music blasted

as the first model, Bubbleisha, strutted down the runway.

"And here eez Bubbleisha looking *très* cool under zee hot sun in her Banana Split Knit," Shady introduced. "*Merci*, Bubbleisha!"

Behind Bubbleisha, the other Shoppies sashayed until all four frozenly fashionable girls graced the runway.

"And I thought ice cream was so last year," Posh Pear said in awe.

"Two words," Handbag Harriet said. "Must. Have."

"Except the cherry vanilla and strawberry," Lippy Lips said. "Too matchy-matchy."

Hearing the applause, Peppa-Mint had such pride for her creations. But suddenly, she saw something that made her gasp: drips of ice cream on the runway!

"Um . . . you guys?" Peppa-Mint squeaked to her friends out of the corner of her mouth. "My ice-cream-sundae hat is melting!"

"You're not alone," Jessicake cried. "Mine is melting, too!"

"Mine is turning into a puddle!" Bubbleisha wailed.

"Oh, no!" Donatina moaned. "My scoops have drooped—all because of the hot sun!"

"And here eez," Shady continued to read—
until she glanced up from her notes and gasped.
"Oh, no! *C'est la* grand meltdown!"

CHAPTER EIGHT

Sip, Sip, Hooray!

Jessicake, Donatina, Bubbleisha, and Peppa-Mint froze on the runway. Their awesome sundae hats were totally ruined—and soon, they would start to overflow!

"This is a disaster," Peppa-Mint moaned.

The girls took off their hats and set them on the runway before they'd be covered in a flood of ice cream. Peppa-Mint sat down next to the bowls, feeling dejected. "After this, the last thing anyone in Shopville will want to do is hang out at Cool Dream," she said sadly. "What have I done?"

"Uhh, Peppa-Mint?" Bubbleisha said carefully. "I hate to burst your bubble even more, but now the ice cream is getting all over the runway!"

She was right—the towering ice-cream sundaes had melted so much that streams of it were now running down the platform.

"Such a mess!" Shady Diva said into the microphone, shaking her head.

"There's only one thing left to do," Apple Blossom declared from the audience. "We've got to drink it up!"

"Huh?" said Peppa-Mint.

Before the Shoppies knew what was happening, Lippy Lips, Posh Pear, Apple Blossom, and the other Shopkins each grabbed a straw from inside Cool Dream and began drinking the melting ice cream from all four hats!

"Mmm!" Kooky Cookie said after emptying half her bowl.

"This is tasty!" said Posh Pear.

"It's more than tasty, Posh," Lippy said with a smile. "The word on everyone's lips is: *delicious*!"

Amazed, Jessicake, Donatina, Bubbleisha, and Peppa-Mint watched from the runway. Soon more and more Shopkins were lining up with straws—even Shady Diva!

"Eez delicious, Peppa-Mint!" Shady Diva exclaimed after taking a sip. "What are zees melted delights called?"

"Called?" Peppa-Mint gulped. "What . . . are they . . . called?"

Peppa-Mint didn't know what to say—but then a small smile spread across her face.

"They're called Melt Shakes!" Peppa-Mint squealed at the top of her lungs, "And you can get them only at Cool Dream Ice Cream Parlor!"

Peppa-Mint realized how loud she had spoken and added softly, ". . . while supplies last."

* * * * *

Just a day later, Jessicake, Donatina, Bubbleisha, and Peppa-Mint had another Girls' Day Out—but this time, it was at the Cool Dream Ice Cream Parlor.

"Look at the turnout!" Donatina gasped as they watched a long line of Shopkins file into the shop.

"Who knew ice cream could be so hot?" said Bubbleisha.

"Thanks to Peppa-Mint," Jessicake praised.

Peppa-Mint blushed as she shook her head. "You mean thanks to *us*," she insisted. "We were an ice-cream team."

"Cookie Dough Melt Shake with chocolate chips, anyone?" Apple Blossom held out a tray as she walked by the girls' table.

"Yes, please!" said the Shoppies. They each took a Melt Shake and sipped happily.

"Most importantly, Peppa-Mint," Bubbleisha said. "We kept you from having another melt-down."

Peppa-Mint smiled, reaching for her straw. "You say *melt* like it's a bad thing!"

LIGHTS, CAMERA, ACTION!

When Popette decides to make a movie of her own—a popumentary about what makes Shopville so great—all of the Shoppies have a different idea of what kind of movie will be the sweetest success. What happens when Popette's movie begins looking less like a popbuster and more like a total flopbuster?

📖 SCHOLASTIC
scholastic.com

SHOPKINS